AF489671

1st Edition | 01
Paperback ISBN: 979-8-9912164-9-4

First Published December 2024

Printed in the USA   1 2 3 4 5 6 7 8 9 10

For inquiries and bulk orders, please email:
indieearthpublishinghouse@gmail.com

Indie Earth Publishing Inc.
| Miami, FL |
www.indieearthbooks.com

INDIE EARTH

FLOR ANA

A CHOCOLATE HOLIDAY

A Novella

AUTHOR'S NOTE

The year is 2023.
Through Indie Earth, I am crafting and creating a story
titled A Chcocolate Holiday, except I'm limited to under
3,500 words and on a tight deadline.

Fast forward one year and, through rock climbing, I meet the
real-life Willy Wonka. After learning about 5150 Chocolate
Co., Tyler Levitetz and I decided to collaborate to
truly bring forth *a chocolate holiday*.

I hope that you enjoy this extended edition of the story and
the chocolates that accompany it.

This is for the readers, for the lovers of chocolate, and for
those who hold sweetness in their hearts despite the
bitterness that life sometimes throws our way.

Here is a sweet treat just for you.

- Flor Ana

"Chocolate is a perfect food,
as wholesome as it is delicious,
a beneficent restorer of exhausted power.
It is the best friend of those
engaged in literary pursuits."

— Baron Justus von Liebig

A Chocolate Holiday

Cocoa Sweets & Carollers

I can't help it. I exhale loudly, gaining a smug look from one of the carollers and I feel my cheeks flush. What I want to do is kick them out, but everyone else seems to be enjoying their merry presence; everyone but me. Unable to handle one more song, and unwilling to be side-eyed once again by the mom carrying her Goldilocks of a child, I head back to the kitchen where the walls are *hopefully* thick enough to block out the cheer.

I enter my cave and comfort, grateful that the carols have become mere whispers in the walls. I take a deep breath, inhaling the sweet smells of sugar and cocoa are my safe haven.

I'm leaning on the counter, about to scroll through my phone, when I hear the kitchen door open, followed by almost noiseless footsteps.

"What are you smiling about, Es?" Sarrie asks.

She's my best friend and business partner-in-crime in opening the only chocolate shop in Moonsville.

I can't help but chuckle, not allowing my resistance towards the holidays and her affinity for it to affect us. Instead, I put my phone down and head towards the fridge for a carton of milk.

"Just the silence is nice."

My smile is cheeky, but there's a silent plea behind it.

"Listen, Sar... I don't know how you talked me into letting those carollers in, and I love you, but next year, it's not happening."

"Sure, Ebenezer. I know you hate the holidays, but our sales have been through the roof–and you know it, too. I mean, what's better than listening to carollers in a chocolate shop while sipping on a nice hot chocolate or indulging in a yummy truffle?"

"Doing any of those things *without* the carollers," I reply a little too bluntly.

A deep exhale escapes me as I prepare myself a cup of coffee.

"Besides," I add, "One of them keeps getting off pitch and the shrill is alarming."

A hearty laugh escapes Sarrie as she goes to steal a sip of my drink.

"Estrella, now I love you, Sweets, but you're the only odd one out here. Everyone else *loves* this—we even had some influencer or reporter—I don't know—out there taking videos. And the squealer... Well, she's only a kid. I think she's like nine," Sarrie says simply, walking back out into the storefront, allowing the shrill of the nine-year-old to once again reach my ears.

As much as it pains me to admit it, I know Sarrie has a point.

Because of the heat waves, Cocoa Sweets Confectionary had been a ghost town in the summer. It was fine with me because, some days, it felt way too hot to even step into the kitchen, but it did make paying the rent of this place slightly more stressful. And even though our signature pumpkin spice chocolate swirls and apple pie brittles had been hits in the fall, the profits and number of customers the carollers have brought in just this week alone is looking to be enough to keep the shop afloat for at least a good chunk of the new year.

Unfortunately *and* fortunately for me, everyone in Moonsville loves the holidays, along with the cold temperatures that accompany them.

Growing up in the hot Nevada desert, and despite having lived in Moonsville for almost 15 years, I guess I've just still never truly adapted to the cold.

The carollers are singing 'Jingle Bell Rock,' and knowing it's the last song in their setlist—unless someone *annoyingly* requests an encore—I'm planning on staying in the kitchen until the carollers are at least a block away.

I'm trying to ignore them, enjoying my coffee, the way my fingertips burn with the warmth of the mug in my hands, the smell of the marshmallow infusion, and the cardamom. A sense of tranquility is washing over me as I hear the distant sounds of applause.

There's a moment of silence.

Ah, finally. Some peace around here.

A smile spreads across my lips as I take another sip, releasing the breath I hadn't realized I was holding. But the peace is short-lived as I hear the words I was dreading, praying I wouldn't hear:

"One more song! One more song!" the holiday-obsessed chocolate lovers cheer, and I can't help but pinch the bridge of my nose and eye-roll as the carollers begin singing 'All I Want For Christmas Is You,' and Mariah Carey would be disappointed with the falsettos of the squealing nine-year-old.

Jesus...

Readjusting in the kitchen office's love seat, I wait out the cheer and doom scroll in my holiday gloom.

Jax Pierce Pressure

*W*ith the carollers gone—and probably disrupting another Grinch's day—I return to the front, pouring milk over hot chocolate bombs for a group of girls that are sitting in the corner booth. I nearly drop the steaming drink tray when I hear a shriek from the kitchen. Quickly, I drop off the hot chocolates, tell the girls to enjoy with an anxious smile, and begin making my way to the back when Sarrie runs out.

I peek over my shoulder to check on the girls but find they've already gone back to their picture-taking, probably TikToking or Instagramming their drinks. Grabbing Sarrie by the elbow, I lead her behind the counter.

"No, Sar. Please. I don't care if Ariana Grande herself is the frontwoman. No more carollers."

Sarrie is smiling *wide*, excitement unable to contain itself in her eyes. Straight up, she looks psychopathic, but it seems the fear in *my* eyes is noted because, without breaking her smile, Sarrie begins to shake her head.

"I promise you this has nothing to do with carollers and you're going to DIE when I tell you what's just happened!" Sarrie screams, regaining the attention of the teens.

I smile in their direction, a hopeful *everything is okay, just enjoy your chocolate, girls*. I can feel my cheeks turning a rosy shade of pink before I take a seat on the countertop, readying myself for whatever Sarrie is about to throw my way.

"Alright, settle down. What is it?" I say in a tone I'm hoping Sarrie will reciprocate.

"Two words: Jax Pierce!" Sarrie shout-whispers.

"What about Jax Pierce?"

"He's coming! To the shop! On Friday!" she sings.

"He's coming *here*? Friday is in two days. Wait, why? Sarrie! Explain."

Sarrie is still smiling from ear to ear, dazed, but at least she's lowered her volume. I can't help it. My nerves getting the better of me as I feel pins and needles in my fingertips. Uncaring for the teenage girls, I shake Sarrie, hoping to get more information out of her, trying to keep my calm at the thought of Jax Pierce in Cocoa Sweets.

He's a chocolatier and god-like at that.

"I just got a call from his team and they want to bring him here to debut a new holiday bar! The dark chocolate marshmallow peppermint honey bar!"

"Oh my god, Sar! This is amazing! So much better than carollers!" Now I'm the one shouting, hugging my best friend for somehow making this happen.

"I know, right? I can't wait to try the dark chocolate marshmallow peppermint honey bar!"

"Please tell me this bar has some sort of name and is not just going to be called the *dark chocolate marshmallow peppermint honey bar...* Because that is a mouthful. Sar, how did you land this?"

Sarrie, ever humble, brushes it off.

"I just submitted Cocoa Sweets to the Chocolatier Chronicle's confectionary directory and told them that we'd be super interested in launching any new treats any collaborating with other chocolatiers!"

"Well, that's... sweet," I say, unsure as to what the Chocolatier Chronicle is but feeling like I should, still mulling over all she's just spewed.

"I may have also said that our store numbers were through the roof and we have over ten thousand followers on social."

Sarrie's blushing while I feel all the color drain from my face.

"What?! What if they find out all of that isn't true?"

The feeling of excitement is short-lived. I can feel the opportunity of meeting Jax Pierce slipping through my fingers.

"What if they call tomorrow and say they're not coming or simply don't show up? What if they call us out for being *liars*?" I add, going to bite my cuticle to alleviate the stirrup of emotions I'm feeling.

Sarrie put her hands on my raised, tense shoulders. I hadn't even noticed that they were almost up to my ears.

"Es, it's only a *half* lie. I mean, look at how packed this place was just a few hours ago. Our store numbers *are* through the roof! And when was the last time you saw how Maddy was managing our socials? We're doing great on there! Sure, we're not at 10k yet, but we'll get there. We'll get there after Jax Pierce comes here, and then we'll be set!"

There's a gleam in her eye as she says it, a level of faith that even *I* could get behind. I also can't help but like the sound of Sarrie's optimism, the chance to get our little chocolate shop on the map. Taking a deep breath, I feel myself strangely relaxed, strangely excited. Now it's my turn to smile wide.

"Ok," I say, hugging the life out of Sarrie, "Let's impress Jax Pierce!"

Nerves & Nuances

*I*t's a quiet morning. Fog rolls down the downtown streets and, for the first time in a long time, I'm finding the cold, chilly air more than bearable. Tolerable. In fact, I find it welcoming. I'm enjoying seeing my breath in the air and the shiver in my fingers as they find their way into my black coat. Morning birds chirp and I can see hints of orange and yellow, hues reminiscent of honey, through the skyscrapers. I'm wearing my favorite blue jeans and a white long sleeve. My hair is freshly washed and I've even applied some mascara and blush.

As I try unlocking the shop door, I can't help but giggle as I notice the shake in my hands. I let out a chuckle as I drop my keys onto the icy sidewalk.

It's been a long time since I've felt so excited about something during the holiday season.

Come on, Es. Get it together, I tell myself, picking up the keys and trying again to unlock the door.

"Oh, for the love of Saint Nick! Give me that!" Sarrie says, startling me.

I hadn't even seen or heard her walk up.

Sarrie grabs the keys from my hand and throws open the doors to the shop, quickly turning on the lights as she makes her way to the counter.

She's wearing black jeans and a cropped pink tank top over a blue long-sleeve, her purple oversized jacket, and a yellow beanie.

I've known Sarrie so long that, just by her walk, I can tell she's nervous—and even if it wasn't for that, the cluster of contrasting colors she's chosen to wear truly gives it away.

Butterflies flutter in my stomach as I look around the shop.

I'm trying to imagine seeing it for the first time and feel joy at the quaint confectionery store Sarrie and I have created. Its vintage anthropomorphic chocolate portraits with their gold frames, the cotton candy walls, the smell of chocolate and sugar, the starry blue rugs placed underneath every table—truly a chocolate shop heaven.

It's all a welcoming dream.

I follow Sarrie to the counter, who is pulling something out of her bag. In a daze, I daydream of what life could be like after Jax Pierce comes to Cocoa Sweets. Of more money coming in to pay employees, more opportunities to attend chocolate-making classes, and taking that longly awaited trip to Belgium. I can feel it. My smile is starlit. I can see it, the future I have long been waiting for...

I catch a glimpse of what Sarrie is holding.

Suddenly, I snap out of it. In Sarrie's hands is an old snow globe.

"What is that?" I ask, my voice conveying more disgust than intrigue.

I had convinced Sarrie that decorating the shop for the holidays wasn't necessary, would clash with the aesthetic we had built, but now with this snowglobe... I'm beginning to think she may have changed her mind and not told me anything about it.

She's smiling manically, and I'm trying my best not to let the little thing in her hand dampen my mood.

"It's my mom's. She gave it to me when I got to Moonsville. Thought it'd bring some good energy to the store for today."

"Oh," I let out, trying my best to ignore the pang growing in my heart.

"Hey," Sarrie says softly. "I know that tomorrow is Christmas Eve and—"

I cut her off quickly, not wanting to know the rest.

"I'm sorry but... What are you wearing?"

Sarrie looks down, letting go of what she was going to say and realizing just how contrasting her outfit is. Laughter bursts from her throat.

"Just pick a shirt," I say through my own laughter.

Sarrie nods, wiping a single happy, nervous tear from her eye.

"Actually, I hate both of these shirts. I don't know why I picked these. Help?" she adds, a high-strung tension settling into her voice.

"Okay," I say, pulling us together, trying to dodge the nerves growing in my chest. "At what time is Jax Pierce coming?"

Sarrie pulls her phone out of her pocket.

"In an hour!" she yelps.

The half-smile I'm sure was on my face dissolves like a hot chocolate bomb in a mug of steamed milk.

Silence fills the room, the only sound the humming of the bakery display showing off the chocolate cakes we'd picked up yesterday in collaboration with a local baker. We both know Sarrie's shirt is a small issue—if an issue at all—but it's easier to focus on it than whatever conversation Sarrie had wanted to have. It's easier to focus on a bad outfit than on who will be walking in through the front doors in an hour.

Sarrie is massaging her fingers, staring down at her mess of shirts as if lost in thought.

At least one of us needs to get our shit together.

I clap loudly, breaking the spell we're both under, if only for a minute.

"Okay," I say, "I may have a shirt in the back office. Go check while I make us some drinks. Jax Pierce will be here soon and... It's going to be great! There's no need to be nervous because everything is going to go great!"

My mindset is very much fake-it-till-you-make-it, but Sarrie nods. With a quick pace, she makes her way to the back while I put on my apron and head behind the bar. Moments later, Sarrie appears wearing my cream-colored sweater.

A sense of calm washes over us, as if, since our outfits are right, things have smoothed and time has frozen.

But before I can even start to think this is the calm before the storm, the front doors swing open.

Letting in the cool air, a woman enters Cocoa Sweets. She wears her hair in a messy bun, a long beige coat over her white jeans and black shirt and pointed stilleto heels.

"Hi, good morning! I'm Rachel Reid with the Chocolatier Chronicle. Are you Sarrie?" she asks, looking at me.

"Actually, *she's* Sarrie," I say, pointing toward my best friend, "but I'm Estrella. Nice to meet you. Thank you again for this opportunity."

"Yeah, no, of course! It's nice to meet both of you! Sarrie really sold us on this place," Rachel says, looking around. "This really *is* a cute chocolate shop! I *love* the whole vibe!"

Rachel's compliment brings in an extra layer of surrealness, somehow making me more nervous *and* excited.

"I hope you don't mind, I wanted to ask you both a few questions before Jax got here, just so we can write about Cocoa Sweets Confectionary on our site."

Sarrie and I can't help but smile at each other, looking forward to our first interview.

Chocolatier Confessions

11 a.m. rolls around and most of our nerves have dissipated into excitement. Guests fill the booths and Sarrie is flowing through the orders, in complete synchronicity with the store. I've just reentered the front with a slice of Peanut Butter Chocolate Heaven to drop off at a table when the room grows quiet.

I don't want to look just yet, but I know it's *him*.

I direct my attention to the front doors, feeling a shiver run down my spine as Jax Pierce and I lock eyes. Before I even have time to let a thought run through my mind, the room redissolving into sound and Rachel is grabbing Sarrie and I, bringing us over to Jax and his team.

"Jax Peirce, this is Sarrie Alba and Estrella Restratta, the owners of Cocoa Sweets Confectionary. Sarrie, Estrella, this is Jax Pierce, and Erin Haug and Logan Les, who are part of his team."

"It's really nice to be here and meet you both," Jax says, extending his hand, his eyes lingering on *me* before they turn to Sarrie's.

I can tell she is trying to keep her demeanor as professional as I am as we shake hands with Jax and his team and lead them lead to the counter.

"Everyone! If I could have your attention for just a moment please," Sarrie begins—and I'm grateful she's the one speaking and not me. "Thank you for joining us today in welcoming a special guest to not only Cocoa Sweets but to Moonsville. Everyone, give a warm welcome to Jax Pierce, who will be unveiling a new confection for you all later today!"

As the crowd of chocolate enthusiasts clap and cheer, more excitement washes over me sweetly.

I can't help but steal quick glances at Jax, his green eyes painting a portrait of paradise I didn't know was possible in its vibrant shade, his black curly hair giving him a sharper edge.

"So, Jax, Estrella will lead you to the kitchen and she'll be your assistant. Erin, Logan, is there anything I can get you guys? Perhaps coffee to go with those cakes."

I had a feeling this would happen given I'm the chocolatier, but I'm still trying to hide my blush as I direct my full attention to Jax.

"You can follow me please," I say semi-shyly, leading him away from the raucous of the front to the quiet peace of the kitchen.

"We got all the ingredients your team requested... I know this is smaller kitchen than what you're used to working in, but I figured we could use the big table as our main table and your photographers can sort of—"

"Oh, there won't be any photographers. I can't concentrate if there's a camera in my face," Jax laughs. "And this isn't small. It's perfect and intimate," he says with a smile, and I can feel the rosiness returning to my cheeks.

Something about him feels so familiar, and yet the closest I've ever gotten to Jax Pierce is liking his videos on social media.

"So, you like getting intimate with small-town chocolatiers?" slips out of my mouth and I immediately regret it. "Sorry! That's not what I meant!"

What the hell, Es?!

Embarrassment is trying to make its way into my gut, but I swear, from the corner of my eye, I think I see Jax smile.

"Actually, no. I meant intimate with chocolate, but perhaps intimate wasn't the right word. Besides, this is actually the first time I'm doing this. I'd been telling Erin that I wanted to work with small stores and it wasn't until now that the idea was sort of approved. In fact, as of right now, it's a one-time thing. A one and done."

"Oh," I say, unsure of *what else* to say, in awe that Cocoa Sweets was the *one selected shop* to run this experience and experiment with.

My brain is a basket of nerves, unraveling one eternal second at a time. I can't deny how much more handsome he is in person, and he seems down-to-earth enough...

I hadn't noticed I was in my own personal bubble, rubbing my hands on the seams of my jeans when I suddenly stop as tinny holiday music begins to play.

My eyes widen, looking around for the cause of my further growing anxiety.

"I used to love these as a kid," Jax says, Sarrie's vintage snow globe in hand.

I've become mute, can feel all the color leave my face as I just stare at Jax Pierce...

"Are you okay?" he asks, setting the snow globe down, genuine concern glossed over his green eyes.

I nod, trying to get my shit together, ignoring the weird feeling wanting to take over my stomach.

"Yeah, sorry. I'm fine. I just... I hate this song."

A chuckle erupts out of Jax.

"How does one hate 'Feliz Navidad?" he asks with a wry smile.

I recluse. "It just reminds me of a time I'd rather forget."

His smile diminishes and I'm kicking myself for admitting this to a stranger. I clear my throat, trying to lighten the mood.

"I'm actually the Grinch... Just without all the green fur," I add.

His smile is back, ever so slightly, and he quickly winds down the snow globe, the remaining jingle sounding rushed and higher pitched as if sung by chipmunks.

"Sorry... I shouldn't have touched that thing," he says awkwardly, rubbing his hands over the front of his jeans before he slides them into his pockets.

He's inched forward, towering me as he gazes into my eyes.

"No, I'm sorry," I blurt out, cheeks flushed and feeling flustered as I take a step back. "It's just... I wasn't expecting to have to deal with that song today. It kind of takes me back to a hard time." I add, crossing my arms, unknowing why I'm even telling him all of this.

No one in Moonsville—except Sarrie—knows my history, what my life was like before Moonsvile, and I intend to keep it that way. Or... I guess, *intended*, because here I am, opening up.

I don't know what it is about Jax Pierce...

But before I can explore the thought further, I feel his warm calloused hand on my shoulder, a look in his eyes as if asking, is this okay?

"Hey," he says, his eyes pouring into mine, "Don't stress it. The holidays are kind of a tough time for me too."

I bite my lip, unsure what to say, trying to keep

the tears from building in my eyes. I divert my attention anywhere else but the green of his eyes. He removes his hand from my shoulder, clearing his throat.

"Look... I don't mean to pry or push onto you my own thoughts, but do know why I'm here today, why I'm *really* here?"

I shake my head.

"To make chocolate with a novice chocolatier and rename a chocolate confection whose current name is quite a mouthful?"

Jax chuckles.

"Not exactly. I'm here because... when I was 18 and just starting out as a chocolatier, no one took me seriously. Until one day, one man did. He was the owner of a small chocolate shop and he brought me on as his apprentice. He taught me everything I know, and gave me the confidence in myself to experiment with flavors that led me to where I am today... Enzo would've been 50 years old today actually, but he got sick... He died three years ago and I... I didn't even get a chance to say goodbye. That's something that haunts me, sometimes, you know? But I still love the holidays and so did he and this is my way of paying it forward. Of connecting with someone that deserves to be shown the confidence that's already within them."

Jax has reclosed the distance between us and now is when I realize I'm the one who has kept pulling away. His eyes are locked on mine, communicating something I can't quite put my finger on.

He continues, "I chose Cocoa Sweets because your friend out there said your dream was to make people feel loved through chocolate. Is that true?"

I nod, looking away, slightly embarrassed.

I can't believe Sarrie told him that...

"I know I just met you, and I'm sorry if this is too forward, but... I don't know... I feel like I know you somehow..."

My breath catches in my throat. I felt it too, this unexplainable connection from the moment he walked in through the door.

Our eyes lock. We both know we should be creating a new chocolate experience for the people outside, but the moment has turned more personal. There seems to be a potential for something else, something more.

"I feel that too," I finally say, a shiver running down my arm as Jax closes the space between us, interlacing his fingers with mine.

"I'm sorry about Enzo," I add, looking towards the floor, breaking the eye contact.

Silence looms over the room as I let out a deep sigh. I don't let my eyes water despite the tears being *right there.* With my eyes still on the floor, I open up my heart.

"I... I lost my mom on Christmas Eve. It was a

few years ago—seven years, to be exact... She was all I had back in Nevada, where I'm from. My dad and I were devastated and I decided to leave home and go somewhere else. I lived in my car for a while until I found Moonsville, or rather, it found me. Sarrie had been my best friend when we were little and I didn't know she was living here. We reconnected and I don't know... One day, we were talking about our dreams and she asked me if I still wanted to be a chocolatier. I thought about it and I did, I still do, and she... Well, she wanted to decorate a store that she could call her own and manage, so we teamed up. But..."

The rest of my sentence dies at my lips. My throat closes, but Jax rubs his fingers over mine as if to say, *It's okay.*

I take another deep breath.

"When my mom passed, I swore I'd never let myself forget it. 'Feliz Navidad' was her favorite song and I don't know... I just made myself hate it, all of it, the whole season... I've forced myself every Christmas to relive the pain of losing her..."

Tears swell in my eyes though I'm still trying to swallow them down.

I do not want to cry in front of Jax Pierce.

My eyes are still glued downward when Jax cups my cheek, pulling my head up to meet his eyes.

"You didn't lose her. Just like I didn't lose Enzo.

They're always right here," he says, putting his hand over his heart.

He's right. I know he is, and I know my mother would be proud to see what I've accomplished. I know she would be ecstatic to know how far I've come.

I nod, letting what Jax said sink into my bones, taking a deep breath. I wipe away a stray tear, letting a shy smile feel its way onto my face.

"This whole time... I should've been appreciating the time I had with her, the love she felt for the holidays. I should've sang that damn song off the rooftops."

Jax smiles. "Well, it's not too late now," he says, walking over to the snow globe to wind it up.

'Feliz Navidad' plays softly, tinny. Jax snaps to the beat, belting out the lyrics in almost-perfect Spanish while maintaining eye contact with me. Laughter finds its way out of my lips and he pulls me close, dancing with me. He smells of chocolate and pine and I try not to melt at the moment.

The experience is something new, something eye-opening and exciting.

The song finishes, and I pull back to meet Jax's green eyes.

"Thank you," I say softly.

"Of course."

Jax clears his throat, a blush taking over his cheeks.

"Estrella..." he starts, but the rest of what he was going to say dies at his lips.

"Yes?" I inquire, my heart skipping a beat in my chest as his eyes stumble on my lips before moving up to meet mine.

I can feel my chocolate irises melting into his green ones. I take a step forward, looking quickly at his lips before I return them to the comfort of witness a galaxy amidst pupils.

"Can I kiss you?" is a whisper he releases breathily and Jax slowly moves his line of sight from my eyes down to my lips.

On instinct, I bite them, trying to contain the rosiness I'm sure is painted all over my face.

"That depends," I say breathily, teasing him. "You out here kissing every chocolatier you meet?"

It's a little forward, my heart wanting to burst and reverse time to swallow the words back down. But Jax just smiles, letting his hand reach for the strands of my hair that have found their way to my face and gently tucking them behind my ear.

"If it's you I'm meeting every time, then yeah."

Amazement burns into my nervous system, yearning for his lips to meet mine. That was not the response I was expecting. It's better than anything I could've thought he would say.

Gently, Jax grabs my cheek and pulls me in, our

lips connecting with a rush of warmth that quickly turns more.

I've been kissed plenty of times before, but this kiss feels different, like sweet magic. If I believed in it, I would say the kiss contains sparks, electricity that seems to vibrate through us both.

Pulling away, I feel lighter, free in a way I haven't in years. Tension has resolved itself in my chest, in my heart, and for the first time in a long time, I'm grateful for the holidays, for 'Feliz Navidad' played out of a tinny snow globe. A chill runs through my body as my brain processes everything that has just happened:

Jax Pierce kissed me. I told him my biggest secret. And I'm about to be his apprentice for the day.

Words cannot describe the emotions that run highways through my veins. A giddy smile appears on my face that can't be removed, even by carollers singing out of pitch.

A sense of peace washes over me, and for the first time in a long time, I feel my mother's presence in the room, all around me. If I believed in it, I would say Jax was sent by her to make things alright again...

Triple Treat

A sweet smell of cocoa coats the kitchen.

Jax has been teaching me his tricks and techniques for quickly tempering chocolate and we keep finding any excuse to touch. A bump of elbows. An around-the-back tutorial on how to sift the cocoa powder onto the lined tray.

We're waiting for the dark chocolate to be finished when I can't help but ask the question that's been on my mind since Sarrie told me Jax was coming.

"So," I clear my throat, "Why the dark chocolate marshmallow peppermint honey bar?"

A smile appears on my lips that Jax seems to reciprocate followed by a chuckle.

"You know, I asked myself that too."

"What do you mean?"

"I thought it was your idea?" Jax says, puzzled.

Now it is my turn to chuckle.

"What? No! I mean, it sounds good, but..." I sigh. "Sarrie."

"Wait why are you sorry?"

"No, I mean SARRIE, like the girl outside who clearly set all of this up."

"Oh...," Jax says, slightly embarrassed.

"It's okay. She's my best friend. She's allowed a few Get-Out-Of-Jail-Free cards, but... Also knowing her, and knowing your ridiculous talent in the kitchen, why don't we make something else instead?"

I can see a sparkle across Jax's eyes as they meet mine.

"I'm listening... What do you have in mind?"

"I... I'm actually not sure. I have a few things in mind."

"Okay, well... We have time. Why don't we test out all of them?"

"What?"

I slap my hands down on the metal table a little too loudly for my taste in shock, in slight terror, but all Jax does is laugh as he leans in and cups my cheek.

"I believe in whatever confectionary treat— treats—you're thinking. I believe in you."

My cheeks warm as my eyes slowly drift to Jax's full lips. And before I know it, they're on mine again, a slight taste of cocoa on his tongue. I pull back with a smile, just enough space for our breaths to mingle still.

"Okay, I believe in me, too..." I bite my lip, unsure of what this feeling is fluttering in my stomach but allowing it to be. "Let's get some white chocolate and milk chocolate going, too. There'll be treats for everyone."

Jax's near-perfect smile is beaming.

"I like the sound of that," he says, leaning in for another kiss before he unpacks his apron from his bag and ties it on.

Never have I felt so inspired. Never have I been so ready to embark on a chocolate-filled holiday.

A Chocolate Holiday

We emerge from the kitchen a few hours later as the sunset paints shadows on the chocolate shop floor. The room falls silent. Long has everyone awaited this moment. It's a chance to make a memory of Moonsville that will outlive us all. One that may bring more chocolate lovers to the city. One that may change lives.

"Well?" shouts someone from the crowd, "Are we eating some chocolate?"

The room fills with soft chuckles and applause, and Jax makes his way over to Logan, giving him the signal to head to the kitchen before taking to the center of the room.

"Thank you all so very much for your patience," he begins, raising his eyes at the man who spoke out with a smile. "We are excited to present to you something a little different, but we can assure you it is simply delicious. Cocoa Sweets Confectionary would like to present you all with... A Chocolate Holiday!"

Logan emerges from the kitchen holding out sets of confections and passes them to Sarrie and the media, then to the guests.

"We were going to deliver just one confection—the dark chocolate marshmallow peppermint honey bar—but we thought we'd deliver something a little... merrier. Estrella, would you mind sharing what we made?"

He turns to me with a smile and I can feel my cheeks turn pink.

"Of course. So... These are all mini, but Jax and I had the vision of selling them in sets of six so you can have two of each confection. First, on the left, is a white chocolate peppermint truffle with crushed candy cane on top. Then, you have a semi-sweet chocolate marshmallow truffle with a honey drizzle. And lastly, on the right is a dark chocolate raspberry coconut swirl. We hope you enjoy."

The crowd dives in, some with professionality and others hunger. I can't help but feel chills as I watch, with glossy eyes, people eating the confections Jax and I made.

I'm on cloud nine, in a chocolatier's heaven, so immersed in taking in everyone's reactions that I barely notice when Sarrie appears next to me behind the counter.

"Es! These are so good!" she says, a wide smile painted on her face, sparkles in her blue eyes.

I can't help it. I pull my best friend into a tight

embrace

"I'm sorry," I whisper into her ear.

Sarrie pulls out of the hug with confusion on her brows.

"Sorry for what, Es?"

I try to bite back the tears that want to pour. Tears of regret, of sorrow.

"The snow globe and the song... Sar, I'm really sorry I've been a jerk *every* holiday season. I promise it stops here. I... Well, I actually had a really nice conversation with Jax and I think I'm ready to let go of this Scroogeness and actually use the season to honor my mom."

Sarrie bites her lips, holding back her own tears. She pulls me into another embrace.

"That's all I've ever wanted for you, Es. Wish it was me who broke you out of this decade-old funk, but instead, it was hunk... Care to share what went down in there?"

I can already feel the blush creeping back up on my cheeks as my eyes move to Jax who is already looking at me. He gives me a wink and my heart slightly melts. I don't know what's to happen next, but I do know one thing: it's only the beginning.

Acknowledgments:

This book truly wouldn't exist without *A Winter's Warmth: Short Stories To Keep Out The Cold* and the love for sweets that has always driven me to embrace the sweet moments of life.

I want to thank Indie Earth for allowing me the reality of slowly making dreams come true and my family for always being so supportive of these dreams. To my friends, thank you for believing in me.

Obviously, I have to thank The Edge Rock Climbing Gym for allowing me to find myself in my mind, body, and soul through movement and strength and for allowing me to meet my good friend and confectionary creative mastermind Tyler Levitetz. Tyler, thank you for collaborating with me to create something sweet that readers and chocolate lovers can enjoy and share with their loved ones.

To my readers, thank you for your support. I know I say this every time, but your love and support are what push me to keep going. Thank you for every chance you give me to move your heart with my words.

To you all, I hope you find this story sweet and the chocolates that accompany it even sweeter.

Other works by Flor Ana:

Perspective (and other poems)

The Language of Fungi & Flowers (A Collection of Poems)

Nourish Your Temple: Self-Love & Care Poetry

A Moth Fell In Love With The Moon (Poems)

The Truth About Love (Poems)

Amanita: A Novel

About the Author

Flor Ana is a Cuban-American writer, singer, and poet who loves to make people feel something through her words. She is the author of a handful of poetry collections, including: *Perspective (and other poems)*, *The Language of Fungi & Flowers*, *Nourish Your Temple: Self-Love & Care Poetry*, *A Moth Fell In Love With The Moon* (which went on to be a finalist for the 2023 American Writing Awards), *The Truth About Love*, and her debut novel, *Amanita*. Flor is also an event poet with her typewriter creating on-the-spot, heart-warming poetry for strangers and loved ones alike using her intuitive energy. She has been the lead singer of alternative rock band Leather & Lace since their start in 2012 and has also released spoken word albums to further showcase her poety and music with the world. When Flor is not writing, she is helping other writers, being creative in any way she can, rock climbing, and indulging in the sweet moments shared with her loved ones through food, travel, and the universe itself and all its delicacies.

Connect with Flor:

Instagram: @littleearthflower
TikTok: @floranawrites

About 5150 Chocolate Co.

Bean to Bar

If you asked a chocolatier whether what I was planning to do made any sense, they would tell you that I was crazy. I know because I asked, and they did.

A skilled chocolatier can create anything from bonbons to a life-sized sculpture of Benedict Cumberbatch, but believe it or not, one thing chocolatiers don't create? Chocolate. The physical act of making chocolate belongs to that of a "chocolate maker." So, in all my years as a chocolatier, not only was I never responsible for actually making chocolate, I barely knew how it was made in the first place.

For something as romantic as chocolate, I always felt that this disconnect left something to be desired. I knew that if I could bring these roles closer together and truly understand what it takes to make great chocolate, I could not only create a product that tastes as good as it looks, I could create a chocolate unlike any you've ever experienced.

This is where things started to go off the rails.

My apartment became a makeshift chocolate laboratory. I used whatever tools I could find to get the job done: juicers, modified lentil grinders, an old book shelf...but we won't get into all of that. After weeks of constant tinkering, I had something that lookedlike chocolate, but tasted horrible.

It wasn't until I began focusing on the cacao itself that I finally realized how I was going to make great chocolate. I discovered that, much like the grapes used to create a fine wine, cacao tells a story. The cacao beans from Madagascar taste acidic and fruity, while the beans from the Dominican Republic are woody with tobacco notes. These subtle nuances are traditionally considered "defects" among the big chocolate companies, and are typically blended together to create a reproducible "house blend." The cacao and the farmers that grow it are an integral part of the process, and neither was getting the respect they deserved.

Good choices, make great chocolate.

Many would say that making your own chocolate is impractical and difficult. Making a chocolate that embraces the "defects" and pays respect to its origins, recognizes its farmers for the skilled craftsmen they are (by paying up to four times the current market price for the finest quality cacao, and empowering them to reinvest in their business and community), is unwilling to sacrifice creativity for profit, embraces and defies tradition, and is equally fueled by science and relentless curiosity? You're right, it is crazy.

Welcome to 5150 Chocolate Co.
Crazy good chocolate.

Connect with 5150 Chocolate Co.

Instagram: @5150chocolateco

About the Publisher

Indie Earth Publishing Inc. is an author-first, independent co-publishing company based in Miami, FL. A publisher for writers founded by a writer, Indie Earth offers the support and technical assistance of traditional publishing to writers without asking them to compromise their creative freedom. Each Indie Earth Author is a part of an inspired and creative community that only keeps growing, making a difference one book at a time. For more titles from Indie Earth, or to inquire about publication, please visit:

www.indieearthbooks.com

For inquiries, please email:
indieearthpublishinghouse@gmail.com

Instagram: @indieearthbooks